ROSA'S PARROT

BY JAN WAHL

ILLUSTRATED BY
KIM HOWARD

WHISPERING COYOTE PRESS

Published by Whispering Coyote Press
300 Crescent Court, Suite 860, Dallas, TX 75201

Text was set in 18-point Goudy Old Style.
Book production and design by *The Kids at Our House*
10 9 8 7 6 5 4 3 2 1
Printed in Hong Kong

Library of Congress Cataloging–in–Publication Data

Wahl, Jan.
Rosa's parrot / by Jan Wahl ; illustrated Kim Howard.
p.   cm.
Summary: Rosa is hard of hearing and she relies on her
parrot, Pico, to repeat things loudly for her, but sometimes Pico takes
advantage of Rosa to create mischief.
ISBN 1–58089–011–3 (hc)
[1. Deaf—Fiction.   2. Physically handicapped—Fiction.
3. Parrots—Fiction.]   I. Howard, Kim, ill.   II. Title.
PZ7.W1266   Ro   1999   98–4776
[E]—dc21   CIP
                                                                      AC

To Cameron
and his brothers
Chase, Chandler, and Noah
—J.W.

For Ketchum, Idaho, my hometown,
and for all my eccentric friends
who continue to make life colorful.
—K.H.

Rosa lived in a little pink house
on a little blue street in a little brown town.

She lived alone with her parrot Pico.
Rosa was hard of hearing.
Every morning at six, Pico woke up. He said,
in a small, quiet voice:

"Little Rose! My chocolate!" He liked hot chocolate.

But Rosa lay in bed sleeping. And
he said, in a bigger voice:
"Rose! My chocolate!"
But Rosa still lay in bed.

Soon Pico shouted:
"BIG ROSE! MY CHOCOLATE!"
At last, Rosa got out of bed and they both had hot chocolate.

One morning, it went like this. There was a
knock on the door.
"Who is it?" asked Rosa.
"Who is it?" shouted Pico.

The man at the door cried, "The man with the milk."

"The man with the milk!" shouted Pico and Rosa bought some.

Later came another knock.

"Who is it?" asked Rosa.

"Who is it?" asked Pico.

The man at the door cried, "The man with the tomatoes!"

Pico hid his head behind a green parrot wing.

"Not today!" he giggled. When Rosa went to the door, the man had left.

"Where did he go? If that was the man with tomatoes, we need some."

And she put her hat on her head. Quiet as
a stone, Pico sat on her hat.
He looked like part of the hat.

Rosa and Pico went off to market. They passed Mayor Flan, who nodded politely.

"Where are you going?" he asked.

"What?" asked Rosa.

"Where are we going?" Pico called.

"To market," said Rosa, smiling back.

"I will go with you," said Mayor Flan. And Mayor Flan, Rosa, and Pico went to market.

They passed Inez the flower woman,
who offered a pretty flower.

"Where are you going?" asked Inez.

"What?" said Rosa.

"Where are we going?" cried the parrot
on the hat.

"To market," said Rosa, smelling the bloom.

"I will go with you," said Inez.

And Mayor Flan, Inez the flower woman,
Rosa, and Pico went to market.

They passed Pepe the violinist, who played a sweet song.

"Where are you going?" asked Pepe, waving his bow.

"What?" said Rosa.

"Where are we going?" called Pico.

"To market," Rosa said.

"I will go with you," said Pepe. "May my dogs go too?"

"Okay," said Pico from the hat.

So Mayor Flan, Inez the flower woman,
Pepe the violinist and his dogs, Rosa, and Pico
went to market.

Rosa stopped at the stall of the egg seller.
Then she stopped at the stall of the tomato
seller. Counting coins.
　　She was about to pay the tomato seller.
Pico sat on her hat.

He looked down at Pepe's dogs.
"MII-YOW!" he called and hid behind his parrot wing.

The dogs were sure it was the market cat.
They raced between the legs of Pepe the
violinist.

Bravely, Pepe held on to his prized violin.
Tomatoes and flowers and eggs flew through
the air—hitting everybody.

Wup! Bomp!
"MII-YOW!" Pico repeated. Laughing
so hard, he fell off Rosa's hat.

Rosa ran home as fast as her plump
legs could carry her.

She unlocked the door and took off her hat.
"Ay, Pico," she sighed sadly. "Such a bad bird.
Go sit in the corner!"
Silently the parrot sat and sat for hours,
his long tail drooping.

At last, in a very small, very quiet voice, Pico spoke:

"Little Rose! My chocolate!"

Rosa said nothing. Then, he said in a bigger voice:

"Rose! My chocolate!"

Still she said nothing. Soon, Pico puffed himself up and shouted:

"BIG ROSE! MY CHOCOLATE!"

"Ay, Pico," laughed Rosa. "What will I do with you?"

The parrot said nothing!
And they both had hot chocolate.